LOST ON TAIKUS

Ian's Realm Saga

D.L. Gardner

Lost in Taikus

This book is a work of fiction. Names, characters, places, and incidents either are works of the author's imagination or used fictitiously. Any resemblance to actual events, locales, or persons, living or dead, is entirely coincidental.

Copyright © 2018 by D.L. Gardner
Special edition @2023
Illustrations generated in MidJourney

INTRODUCTION

Hacatine, the wicked sorceress queen of Taikus sailed the high seas in search of the four young wizards, Silvio, Kaempie, Meneka and Reuben, seeking to rob them of their magical powers and use it to conquer the lands of the North. When the four wizards split up, Reuben was able to return to the island and rescue his sweetheart Lelanie who had just given birth to Reuben's son. Abbott. Hiding in a cave surrounded by Hacatine's warrior women. Reuben bartered with the gypsies from the Isle of Refuge, promising them the use of his magic for a safe return to their island, and a place for him and his family to live free from the tyranny of Hacatine's kingdom.

When Hacatine returned to Taikus after a grueling shipwreck and unsuccessful venture, *(Tale of the Four Wizards)* she spent much of her time replenishing what she had lost. Once her fleet was restored, she re-established the search for the missing wizards. Word came to her that Reuben was now living on the south side of the Isle of Refuge; a port well protected by the King of Alisubbo, whose royal navy patrolled the channel. She dared not venture into the king's territory, having lost many ships and a portion of Taikan shoreline in a war. Instead, Hacatine sent scouts to spy out Reuben's location and bring her news. When she discovers Reuben's charms have been compromised, but that the wizard has a son, a boy with magical powers, she makes plans for the boy's abduction.

LITTLE WIZARD

The fur that hung from the woman's belt smelled musty and rancid, much like the bones Auntie Rosalind would toss to the dogs. Abbott turned his head away and wiped his nose. He hated that smell. The woman on his left jerked his wrist.

"Keep up," she said, dark eyes resting on his auburn hair, for she towered well above his eye level. "Little wizard!"

"I could keep up if you didn't walk so fast. My legs aren't as long as yours. You've already captured me. Why do you rush?" The Isle of Refuge was a long way away now, and Auntie Rosalind would worry more about him than she would their pet dogs. If she had any idea that these women were pushing and shoving him around like this, she'd cast a spell on them they'd never forget.

The woman they followed slowed, looking over her shoulder first at him, and then his tormenter. "The boy's right Deanna. Hacatine won't be in the hall just yet. We have time."

Deanna sneered. "How could a boy be right, Justine? You must be joking!"

"He's not just a boy. He's magic. This is Reuben's son, remember?"

Abbott shot a glance at the woman named Justine. "How do you know my father?"

"She doesn't," Deanna blurted, rudely. "Only by rumor. Hacatine has an Act-of-Revenge to settle with your father, and I'm afraid you are part of her plan." The seriousness of Deanna's voice sent a chill down Abbott's spine.

Revenge was an act both his mother and father taught against. *"A wizard's magic can do many evil things if it's not contained. Our gift should be wielded in love, not hate, not revenge,"* his father once told him.

Abbott held his tongue after that as he followed the warrior women up the hill. Edged on the bank overlooking the sea stood the castle. So white were its walls that Abbott had to squint to keep the glare from burning his eyes. With pillars that reached for a turquoise sky, the fortress both guarded the island and lauded its magnificence. Stairs leading to the entry were wide and began halfway down the bank. It took two steps and a jump for Abbott to climb each one. So concentrated was he in keeping with his escort's pace, he nearly missed seeing the lion statue that heralded the entry way. If he hadn't been forced to keep moving, he would have stared at the proud creature for a much longer while. Cats, big or small, were a favorite of Abbott's. He had a way with animals. He even brought home a baby bobcat he found by the river once, though Auntie Rosalind made him take it back. Bobcats never got this big, though. Perhaps his captors would allow him to return to the giant stairs and let him enjoy the lion statue another day.

Once at the entrance, the women halted, giving him a chance to marvel at the etchings on the door. Tall ships, a rocking sea and a moon decorated the entryway where they waited. He stared at the engraving as Deanna clapped the knocker.

"It tells a story!" Abbott said and then smiled up at the women. "I can read it!"

With a loud squeak, the doors opened, and a stream of cold air hit his face.

"Yes. It does." Justine riffled his hair, and then quickly pulled her hand away when they passed the tower woman. The sentry's armor flashed a beam of light as Abbott walked by, but the guard stood rigid, a sullen expression on her face.

The floor felt hard and flat under Abbott's bare feet, unlike the sandy beaches that tickled his toes just a few hours ago, and unlike the forest, mulch that gave way under his soles. He had never walked on anything this hard before. Not even the granite stones in the ancient ruins on his island felt this cold. The halls were made of the same smooth surface; so shiny he had an urge to run and touch them, but the grave expression on his escorts warned him not to. The eight-year-old had never seen walls like these before. Colorful plates reached to the ceiling with images of flowers carefully painted, their leaves like lace tickling a background of coral and yellow. "Do flowers that look like this exist in real life?" he asked.

"Yes, they do. Though we haven't seen any blooms for a long time," Justine whispered with a frown. "Blossoms are a sign of peace, one thing Taikus has no memory of."

"Our island is at peace." There was pride in Abbott's voice. He loved his home and the quiet life he lived. Deanna looked at him with scornful eyes. Abbott cleared his throat. "Was," he added with a grimace, his eyes narrowed.

"If your father plans on rescuing you, he'll be in for a big surprise."

"You'll be the ones surprised! My father can do mighty things."

"Can he, little wizard?" Deanna snickered as she glared at him, her distaste for children evident. "Mightier than the sorceress Hacatine?"

Abbott shrugged. He knew better. No wizard alone is mightier than the wicked queen of Taikus.

Abbott was a baby when his mother and father fled from her clutches. He had heard the tales of what the queen did to wizards. Not many had survived her greed for power. Those that did left the island to live with the gypsies on the Isle of Refuge. The only enemy that ever-matched Hacatine came from the fortified city south of the Isle of Refuge, Alisubbo. The king of that township had a fleet, which could shake the earth and cause significant damage to enemy ships. More than once, Alisubbo's vessels aided the gypsies. Abbott couldn't recall ever having met a citizen from that city, so he never understood why the king protected their little island. But his family and the gypsies were grateful for Alisubbo's help.

"When you stand before the queen, bow and then fall on your knees." Deanna's steps quickened as they passed large empty rooms dotted with gilded vases as tall as Abbott. Brilliant red tapestries sheeted the floors, and long vertical windows hung open, ushering in a cool draft of fall air. "Don't look at her. Keep your head down. My guess is it's not her plan to harm you right now."

Abbott swallowed the lump in his throat. The closer he was to the hall of the great queen, the harder his heart throbbed until his chest rocked from its weight and his breath was short.

"I didn't do anything wrong," he mumbled.

"I know." Justine whispered and squeezed his hand.

Abbott would have searched her eyes for the kindness her touch offered, but at that moment the doors to the throne room flew open. He was rushed forward by the queen's attendants and brought to the center of the room.

"Kneel," someone said. Abbott's knees met the floor, and he bowed his head.

Then there was silence. He wanted so badly to look up, but he was too afraid. He could see the warriors' sandaled feet step away from him. The spears and swords tapped the floor at the same time. He smelled the thick odor of liquid flowers on flesh as someone approached.

"This is the magic boy?" a raspy voice asked. "You better not have deceived me."

"This is the one you've been wanting, your highness. None other. I swear by my own life." That was Deanna's voice.

Abbott felt fingers playing with his hair. The woman by his side laughed. Her black skirt brushed his shoulder.

"He's mine now! And for the next ten years, I get to enjoy my revenge. Oh, I'm going to like this. Jolene, bring Claudia."

Claudia? Abbott had heard that name before. He peeked from under his hair when Hacatine moved from his side. An older peasant woman had been brought into the room. The witch queen approached her. Abbott pretended not to look, but he could tilt his head just enough to see Claudia on her knees across the room.

"Look what we have for you, Claudia! A son! You were so adamant about hiding your boy that I've replaced him. I'm giving you the opportunity to raise this little wizard child as your own."

The woman's large blue eyes were gentle but weary. Dark circles shadowed them, and locks of curly gray hair hung disheveled in front of them. But there was gentleness in the look she gave Abbott.

"Why would you be so generous?" Claudia's words were met with a heckle from the queen.

"Why do you think? So that when he comes of age, you can witness his fate in the same manner you should have witnessed your own son's fate. Remember Silvio, Claudia? The one you abetted?"

"I will never forget my son."

"No. No, you won't." Hacatine laughed and waved to her guards. Abbott was pulled to his feet, Claudia shuffled to his side and when they were escorted out of the throne room, Claudia took his hand and held it tight. The warmth of her palms took his fear away.

He walked with her down the hallway to the double doors he had come through, Justine and Deanna leading the way.

Sentries stood by the castle entrance with eyes fixed on nothing. They held their lances with firm fists as he passed. Only one woman made eye contact with him, but he couldn't read what she was thinking. Sorrow maybe, but the moment was too fleeting. The sun inched past the horizon, changing the color of the world to autumn gold, like the leaves that fall along the creek where the salmon run.

Just this morning Abbott had been there with his uncle. Just this morning, he'd heard his family crying for him as the skiff rowed away from his home. Abbott searched the narrows in the distance as he followed Justine and Deanna to the houses below the castle. Perhaps he'd see a boat coming for him. Maybe his father would arrive soon. Or maybe his rescuers would wait for nighttime and sneak into the city.

Claudia led him to an adobe house with a garden gate and a cobblestone walkway. Flower boxes decorated the windows, but they were empty. Straw from the thatched roof hung over the eaves. Roses grew along the clay walls, but they were only thorn bushes. No flowers decorated their foliage. Justine and Deanna stepped aside so that Claudia could open the door.

"You'll report daily. Hacatine's orders." Deanna announced, standing at attention.

Claudia took Abbott by the arm and pulled him inside behind her. "I'll take good care of this child. No harm will ever come to him," she whispered, her eyes challenged the warrior women.

After a moment's silence, Justine spoke equally softly. "He could not be in better hands. But we've orders to keep you in check and if you flee or try to rescue him, you won't succeed. We'll find you. We're watching."

Abbott looked to see how Claudia took that threat, but she only smiled and nodded, closing the door gently. "Goodnight."

Alone with the old woman, Abbott absorbed his surroundings. The setting sun had darkened the room, and an evening chill was already setting in. Claudia lit a lantern and set it down near the fireplace where a pile of kindling lay. She picked up a stick and pushed aside the ashes, uncovering a small pile of glowing embers. Once she had stacked the wood carefully on the coals, the room filled with fragrant smoke, and soon flames claimed their fuel. Claudia dusted her hands on her apron, stood and faced him. Immediately he the magic stirred, and he could read into her spirit through her eyes.

"There are clothes in the drawers that belonged to my son. Too big for you, but you'll grow into them. The tunics should fit well enough to stay on your shoulders, and you can roll up the pant legs and tuck them under the boots he used to wear. It looks as though your feet are as big as his were just before he left."

Abbott curled his toes, conscious of her eyes on them. "Silvio knew my father, didn't he?" Abbott asked. He had a peculiar sense that he was suddenly living in his father's stories. The grand island Taikus, the wicked witch queen, and now Silvio's mother—all a part of the legend he had heard time and time again.

"Yes, he knew Silvio. And I knew your father. How is Reuben? It was I that sent them away, you know?"

Abbott shrugged, a wave of homesickness gushing through his gut. She pulled her shawl over her shoulders and walked to the fireplace. "Never mind. A touchy subject for you. I feel the same way about my boy, too, you know? Not a day goes by that I don't miss him."

There was something healing in her voice, even though at that moment they were both feeling the pain of loss. Abbott walked to the fire and stood beside her. "I'll be ready when my father comes to get me. He'll rescue you too."

When the woman's sullen blue eyes met his, Abbott saw her past. It was like watching his father's life happen in front of his very eyes. His father Reuben, Silvio and two other wizards were leaving Taikus. They pushed a skiff into moon lit waters.

"That's the night they escaped, isn't it?" Abbott asked.

Claudia nodded. "You have the same magic that your father has, though he was never very good with it. Never knew when to use it, or how it could benefit him."

"Father got better. He told me how hard being a wizard was. My mother and the gypsies helped him teach me how to control my vision. Still, it comes and goes."

"Keep it secret."

Abbott nodded and sat on the soft couch that faced the fire, his body weary from tension and the physical exertion of the day.

"No matter what happens, and if your father never finds you, it would be best if you think of me as your mother. Living here will be difficult for you otherwise." Claudia sat next to Abbott and combed his hair with her hands. She sighed and then squeezed him tight. "I know it's hard and that you miss your family."

Abbott fought the weak feeling inside that made him want to cry. "One thing my father taught me was to see good in whatever happens." He patted her hand. "The Isle of Refuge isn't all that far. I'm sure we'll escape, and I'll take you with me. My father will be proud to have you live with us and with the gypsies."

Claudia didn't answer him but watched the flames in the fireplace for a long time. Finally, she stirred and took his hand. "I'll show you to your room."

Abbott followed her through a door into a small bedroom. A thick woven blanket with intricate patterns and tiny figures of winged creatures laid spread over the bed and an inviting pillow sat on top. It looked comfortable. More comfortable than his own sheepskins spread over pine needles back home.

"Silvio's clothes are in this trunk. You can try them on in the morning. Silvio had some toys. He said they are important tools of trade. Whatever they are, they're magic things he used to play with. They're in the box under the window. You, being a wizard, are welcome to use them, but put them back when you're done, please."

Abbott stared at the box. The lid was leather and a moon with a face was tooled in the center. It looked worn, as though its owner had given it much use, the leather oiled from handling and a few stitches loose at the seams.

"You should sleep now, though. You've had a long, hard day. Perhaps things will seem better for you in the morning."

Abbott was too tired to argue. He walked to the bed and let her tuck him under the covers. When he was warm, she stood back and looked at him, starlight radiating onto their faces. With a heavy sigh, she leaned over and kissed him on the cheek. An aura of yellow fell softly from her just before he closed his eyes. Claudia was a sorceress, and she was giving him a touch of her magic.

THE GREAT ESCAPE

The house was quiet when Abbott woke. He slipped out of his covers and peeked out the window, looking for the dove that he heard. The bird must have been far off, for all he saw were stars sparkling in between the aspen branches that shifted in the breeze. The sky was turning blue on the horizon. It will be day soon. He had slept through the deep hours of night.

He gasped in fear. What if his father had come during the night and couldn't find him? He should have been more vigilant.

Abbott raced out of his bedroom as quietly as he could so as not to wake Claudia. When he slipped outside, the cool of dawn numbed his face and cold cobblestones chilled his bare feet. He didn't care about the cold. He ran toward the beach–toward the sea—toward home.

Combing the edge of the bank among the willows, Abbott found the trail that descended to the shore. No one had seen him leave. He was free! He would steal a boat and row home. He was getting away. This was easy!

The trail led through a thicket at the bottom of the embankment. Not a well-traveled path. Reeds and grasses pricked at his feet and towered over him, hiding him. When he came to a clearing, he halted, and his heart stilled. Warrior women were everywhere on the beach, standing around campfires, keeping guard over the skiffs, and patrolling the shoreline.

Abbott took a deep breath and stepped forward, surveying the scene–his mind spinning solutions as fast as he could blink. He resisted his fear. His father, his mother, Rosalind, and the gypsies taught him to be courageous. With his head high, he walked to the nearest dinghy and shoved it toward the water.

"Hey!" someone yelled. Several women ran toward him, but he didn't stop pushing the boat. He looked up briefly. They were drawing their bows and aiming their arrows at him. The boat was heavy and took everything he had in him to budge.

"Abbott!" Justine's voice rang out as she sprung from the shadows. "Abbott, little fellow, don't do that!"

He felt a tear roll down his cheek. Though he pushed with all the strength that was in him, instead of sliding on the surface, the skiff had dug into the sand, stuck.

Justine kneeled next to him and grabbed his shoulders gently. "Don't move. They will shoot. Just stand still and talk to me."

"This is wrong." Abbott squinted at her, his gaze dashing over her shoulders at the archers. Two of them broke rank with the others and approached.

"I know." Justine wiped the tears from his cheeks with her thumbs. "I know. It isn't right."

"Then why are you a part of it?" He caught her eye, his magic slowly spiraling into her past. She shook her head for an answer, still allowing him to enter her mind.

"You're all captives, aren't you?" Abbott asked as the other women gathered nearby. "All of you are being used. You've let the wicked queen control your mind. Why?"

Justine's didn't answer, though her lips moved, and he could read them.

"Well, she isn't going to control me. I'm leaving." Abbott straightened, fearless.

"Don't try it, little wizard." Deanna said.

"Why not? Why can't you just let me go? What will the queen do to you if I escape?"

"She'll kill us. We took oaths to protect her and this island."

"I will not hurt your stupid island."

Deanna slung her bow on her back. "Go back to Claudia. She's in danger because you snuck away. Don't think she won't go unpunished. And be thankful we don't drag you to the queen's dungeons as we would any prisoner we catch trying to escape. We aren't going to let you go. Neither will we let Reuben set foot on these shores. And if it makes you feel any better, your father was here last night. Our archers drove him away."

Abbott swallowed. "My father was here. See! I told you!"

"I'll walk you back home." Justine stood and took his hand. "C'mon. Claudia is a superb cook. She'll have something warm for your belly."

Were there not words from the past, advice that his father might have for him in a moment like this? He tried to recall, but nothing came to mind. He was defeated, as simple as that.

"We can pass by the steps of the castle and stop by the great lion. How does that sound?" Justine nodded, her words breaking the tension as she spoke. "C'mon."

18

Abbott's shoulders fell. "No. I don't want to see the lion today." His face grew long as he turned and walked away from the beach.

***

He wasn't lacking hugs from his adopted mother when he returned. He let her squeeze him and ruffle his hair. She served him a healthy breakfast, though he had no appetite. When he set his spoon next to his bowl, she didn't protest.

"Abbott, just try to adjust to our way of life. Don't run away." She cleared her throat with a cough and covered her mouth, tapping her lips. "It's best that way."

Abbott stared at his food. It was unlikely that he'd try to escape again. Maybe when he gets bigger. Maybe when he's strong enough to push a dinghy out of the sand.

"She called for you this morning." Claudia said.

Abbott knew who 'she' was. Wood in the fireplace popped and sparks floated up the chimney. The flames dance lazily over the wood.

"Did you hear me?" Claudia asked.

"Is she going to hurt me?"

"It depends on what you consider pain." Claudia slid his bowl into hers and rose from the table. "She'll try to make you feel bad for what you did."

Abbott shrugged, still watching the fire. "I don't. I would do it again if I thought I could get away. I want to go home."

"Those are natural feelings for a boy your age. But Hacatine doesn't care about our feelings. She is brutal, and you are living dangerously. You must understand your enemy."

He looked up at her. Hacatine was the last person he wanted to know anything about. He hated her. Claudia ignored his scowl.

"Never let on that you're weak, but neither let the queen know your intentions. There are some things she doesn't need to know."

"Why do the warrior women protect her? Can't they see that everything she does is bad? Why doesn't Taikus just rise and overthrow her and be rid of her for good?"

Claudia poured water in a basin and set the bowls to soak. Wiping her hands, she turned to him. "The warriors are more than women, Abbott. They are sorceresses. They once had enough magic to defend themselves from tyranny like hers. But Hacatine robbed them of their gifts, and because of that, she controls them. You understand their powers make her what she is."

"Is that why you don't want me to use my magic? You're afraid she might take it?"

"Hacatine knows you have powers, and she plans on taking them. She wants me to nurture you until you're mature, and then she plans on robbing you. If she doesn't see you use it, she may not covet your magic so much." She gazed out the window. "It could be an advantage for you. Maybe she'd give up and forget, thinking you're just a normal boy." She shook her head solemnly. "Something very evil happens when a sorceress and a wizard's magic mix if it isn't done voluntarily. Hacatine thrives on that evil." She stared out the window, a faraway and saddened look on her face.

"Are you thinking about Silvio?" he asked her.

"Yes," she whispered.

He had no words to make her feel better.

Her eyes were gentle when they rested on him. "I will do anything to keep you safe from her."

"What does she do?"

"She strips the magic from a wizard's soul and then leaves the poor victim to die."

Abbott's heart skipped a beat. "She should be stopped!"

"Yes, Abbott. She should."

"Is it even possible? Isn't she immortal? My father told me once that sorceresses never die."

Claudia shrugged and kneeled by the fire, poking the embers with a stick and then setting a log on the coals. "Sorceresses live for a very long time. Some people say that they, and wizards, are immortal if they never bear children. I don't know if those rumors are true or not. But I know that Hacatine never bore a child."

"I would pity the child if she did! What a horrible life he would have!"

Claudia glanced at him.

"Why is she so bad? Doesn't she think about the things she does?"

"The reason she is evil is as ancient as the mountain to the north. Her desire for power is so strong it makes no difference to her what she does to people." Claudia rose and unfolded a fleece from a stool and handed it to Abbott. "It's cold outside. Wear this. If we don't leave now, she'll send her warriors looking for us. It's always better to come on our own. That way, we can arrive in peace. There's no need for violence. Are you ready?"

Abbott stood. He was as ready as he'd ever be.

Voices met them when he stepped out the door and looked beyond

Claudia's fence to the thatched houses that lined the cobblestone road near to them. Three boys Abbott's size played tag in the street. Bundled in woolen coats, they ran in circles, chasing each other until one collapsed, bringing his friends to their knees next to him in a fit of laughter. Abbott smiled, but Claudia took his hand.

"Come!"

"Can I play with them when I get back?"

"No, Abbott, you cannot play with the young men in the village."

She mumbled into her scarf, but he heard her plainly and shot her a glare. "Why not?"

Claudia wasn't going to answer him, and it left his stomach feeling uneasy. He had thought she was nice.

The fog burned off by the time they came to the great stairway. The day was sunny, but an icy breeze stung his cheeks. Claudia wrapped her shawl tighter around her neck and lifted the fleece over his head. Abbott blew a puff of breath just to see the steam.

"Look! It's like a dragon's breath." He grinned at her. "Can we look at the lion before we go inside?"

Without a word, she led him toward the statue at the top of the stairs. Even though she walked slowly, he still had to leap over the steps to keep up. But the chilly morning gave him fresh energy. He would have run circles around Claudia if the large gold cat statue, its mouth open, teeth catching the morning rays, hadn't distracted him. Not until he was next to it did Abbott realize how tall it stood. Cool to the touch, he ran his fingers over its sculptured paw. "Are lions really this big?"

"Perhaps." Claudia put her arm around his shoulders. "I wouldn't know."

"Why is it here?"

"Well, little wizard, I guess the reason they put this statue on the steps of the castle is because lions are king of their kind. They signify royalty."

Abbott looked up at the woman. Her eyes cast the same blue as the sky behind her. Her lips turned up slightly, but they quivered, maybe from the cold.

"If this is a royal palace, and he guards the castle doors, then there should be a proper king." Abbott smiled at the thought. "Wise and strong. Like this lion."

Claudia nodded. "That would be a good thing, little wizard. Let's go inside, Abbott."

CONSTANCE

Abbott's walk to the castle with Claudia wasn't as frightening this time as it had been the first day he kneeled before the queen.

"I don't care if she's mad at me! What does she expect when you steal someone away from their family?" Abbott held his head high as he walked through the hall. "I'll stand up to her. I'll ask her why she thinks she can kidnap me."

"Easy young one." Claudia's hand rested on his shoulder. "Her bite is worse than her bark. You can think whatever you want, but those thoughts should stay in the confines of your mind. You cannot fight her by yourself. Should her wrath come against you, even I can't help you."

Justine and Deanna appeared in the entryway to the throne room. Deanna blockaded them from entering, holding her lance out, signaling them to halt. "Raise your hands and let us search you." Justine took the shawl from Claudia and shook it, searched the woman's pockets and brushed her fingers through the old woman's hair.

"Abbott." Deanna took Abbott's chin and lifted his head. "The queen gives her prisoners three chances and three only. As much as she wants you to reach the age of eighteen, if you give her trouble, she'll take your life."

The eye contact gave Abbott a chance to use his magic and dive into Deanna's past.

"What will she do with my life once she takes it?"

Deanna's face turned red.

"I'm not afraid of Hacatine," Abbott's voice sounded more like his father's than his own. I see you are. But I'm not." Amazed at the tenacity of his own words, his heart thumped in his chest. "And you can go back to your home in the woods anytime you want. In fact, go back. Your mother is there crying for you to come home."

Deanna drew her hand away. "What do you know about my mother?" She gasped. Fear made her body tremble. "You're using your magic! What did you see?"

"You." Abbott smiled to himself. "Just you."

"Let's go," Claudia took his hand and pulled him away, leaning near to his ear as they walked. "Don't use your magic on these people. They tell everything to Hacatine."

"Sorry." Abbott mumbled, but he only apologized to calm Claudia. He wasn't sorry. He had seen into Deanna's life and now knew why she acted the way she did.

The floral tiles and arched windows lit the way down the hall again, echoing every step they took. Claudia hurried, but Abbott fell behind. His gaze wandered over the architecture that dwarfed him. Morning light shone softly through the stained glass, spotlighting the fauna in the vases and sending spots of light that danced on the rugs.

There was movement under the window that they passed. A shadow, much larger than the figure it came from. A young girl sat with her back to the hall. Her body swayed back and forth in rhythm and he thought he heard her hum, but Claudia grabbed his hand again and rushed him forward to the queen's throne room.

"Let's get this over with," she said.

The double doors were open wide. This time Abbott got to see the grandeur of the queen. Two pillars coated in pure gold framed a pathway lined with red carpet. Above them hovered a ceiling painted with gargoyles and winged creatures. In the center of the room, on a throne of dark wood, sat the queen. A canopy of velvet surrounded her. Women waited on her, waving huge fans made from feathers of birds Abbott never knew existed. Hacatine was an amazing sight. Long silver hair fell over her shoulders. Her skin was pale, her eyes gray with long white lashes. She wasn't a homely person. In fact, Abbott considered her beautiful. Her gown was a deep blue with tiny prisms sparkling from the light that shone through the window. The attendants were not warriors, for they didn't wear any armor, but graceful ladies dressed in balloon pants and silky tops. Beads adorned their hair on their armbands and around their necks. The lady smiled at him when he entered, and he smiled back. The other women moved away from the queen.

"Oh yes, the runaway." Hacatine sat erect in the chair and held out her hand for Abbott and Claudia to stop. "That's far enough. I can smell you already and it's not a pleasant odor." She snapped her fingers and nodded to one of her aides. The girl came up to Abbott with a bottle, spraying a misty perfume of mint and lilac over him. Abbott waved his hands in the air and coughed, ending his protest with a sneeze. The queen laughed.

"Well, I suppose that's a bit much for a little boy." She stood, her grin ironing into a frown. "Claudia, you disappointed me to no end. I trusted you and look what you've done. I thought you'd keep this rascal in line."

"Your highness, the boy's heart is broken. Give him time."

"I intend to give him time!" Hacatine's response was quick and curt. "I intend to give him ten years. It's up to you to make certain he lives that long. I'm not here for kinder care. That's your job. Raise that boy and make certain his magic is nurtured. Do you understand?"

"Yes, your highness." Claudia bowed low and took Abbott's shoulder to gain her balance.

"And whatever you do, keep him away from the beach, the boats and the water." She made a face and waved her hand under her nose. "Not the bath water, though. Make sure he has plenty of that." The queen's attendants laughed.

Abbott's stomach soured, and his face heated. "You'll be sorry if you try to keep me here for ten years," he said.

The queen pivoted around; her smirk biting the air as she showed her teeth in disdain. "Oh? You think? How so, little wizard? Are you threatening me?"

Abbott shook his head. "No. I just think you might be sorry that I'm here. You might decide it isn't good for your island."

"If you're referring to your father and his silly little army coming to attack us and take you away, I assure you, they pose no threat to me! And if he comes around again, we might even capture him. That little head of yours couldn't imagine how long I've been wanting to get my hands on his powers."

Abbott tried to catch the queen's eyes, but the woman wouldn't focus on him. "He's more powerful than you think!" he said.

"Powerful? Ha! Don't talk to me about power, little one. You do not know what genuine power is. If you did, you'd hold your tongue. I…" she took a step toward him, smirking as she walked. "Have enough power to make you hate your father and despise your mother forever giving birth to you. I'll be more than happy to give you a brief sample of what my power can do!" She snickered and flicked her hair over her shoulders. "But honestly, you're hardly worth the effort. Maybe when you get older. Now, go away. You bore me. I don't need to waste my time with you. Claudia," she pointed at the old woman. "This is your only warning. I won't be so kind to either of you if this rascal tries to escape again." She sneered at

Abbott. "Broken heart. Pfft!"

One attendant shuffled them out of the room. Abbott would have run if it weren't for Claudia grabbing his hand in the hallway.

"You're too bold, Abbott. What makes you think you can talk to her that way? You're going to get us both in trouble. Is that what you want? Do you want a flogging? Or have me tortured? She does you know." Claudia mumbled and scolded as they hurried toward the exit, but Abbott had already lost interest. The girl he had seen earlier was standing by a marble pillar, watching them approach. When their eyes locked, it stilled his anger. Her long hair fell over her shoulders, white as the ocean breakers on a windy day. She couldn't have been any older than Abbott. Her skin was pink, her eyes blue, and her feet bare. She wore a simple white dress with a colorful scarf tied around her waist. A scowl darkened her face. She stepped back when they passed, still staring. Instead of continuing, Abbott stopped.

It was easy to see into her mind. She was an orphan. There was some violence in her past, and an ocean voyage. She didn't respond to his mind reading, which made Abbott think maybe she didn't know he was looking into her. Sorceresses always knew, but this girl didn't. She could very well be a human.

"Who are you?" she asked.

"I'm Abbott."

"The prisoner?" She tilted her head in curiosity.

He didn't answer.

"The magic boy?"

Claudia had stopped her ranting and turned, but she didn't interrupt them. Abbott shot her a questioning look. No one was supposed to know about his magic. "Why do you ask?"

"Are you staying with Claudia in the village?" The girl's grimace eased when she glanced at the old woman.

"Yes," he said.

"Then you are the Magic Boy! I know where Claudia lives. My name is Constance. Do you want me to come and visit you sometime?"

After checking Claudia for permission, he smiled at the thought of having a friend. "That would be fun."

"Good. I'll come and see you when my morning spinning is done."

"Spinning?"

"Yes! Spinning!" She laughed and twirled. The wind lifted the hem of her dress over her bare feet. Breathless and catching her balance, she finished her dance and faced him again. "No, silly. Not that kind of spinning. Raftal!"

"What's raftal?"

"Something I gather in the forest. It's my secret. No one knows where it comes from except me. That's why they keep me. I spin raftal into yarn and then the attendants dye it and weave it into cloth for the queen's wardrobe." She nodded toward a neat ball of silky yarn resting on a table under the window. "You saw her beautiful clothes, didn't you?"

"I guess." The queen's clothing was not something Abbott had been interested in. He had been more amazed at the painted gargoyles on the ceiling and the real armor hanging from the walls.

"Well, I don't mind showing a magic boy where my gathering place is."

His grin grew wide. "I would like that!"

"Good. Later this afternoon."

"Come on, Abbott. Let Constance finish her work." Claudia took his hand and Abbott eagerly followed, looking forward to the afternoon.

On the way home, a warm feeling inside kept his spirits up. "Claudia, mum?" he started, unable to form the question that was bothering him.

"Yes, Abbott, son." She flashed him a warm smile.

"It's all right if I spend time with this girl?"

"Yes. You may spend time with her."

"Then why can't I spend time with the boys on our road?"

Claudia sighed deeply and tightened the squeeze on his hand. "The boys on our road are boys, not wizards, like you. Mingling with the villagers would not be a healthy idea. It's forbidden."

"Why not? I just want to play?"

"But the play would turn to questions. Answers would bring sympathy. It's hard to say what the citizens would do for your sake. Hacatine cannot risk a rebellion. She would use violence to squash it. I forbid that to happen. I don't want to see anyone get hurt, Abbott, especially not a child."

***

When they returned to Claudia's house, the woman made lunch for the two of them. She gathered the vegetables that Abbott chopped into cubes and wrapped them into flatbread, sprinkling the sandwiches with goat cheese. Abbott gobbled his food quickly and took his plate to the basin, washing all the dishes that had been piled on the counter.

"My, you're working hard this morning!" Claudia laughed as she set the last wooden bowl in the cupboard. Abbott dried his hands.

"I want to get the chores done quickly."

Claudia laughed. "Why? Because you have a pretty little friend coming over?"

Heat rushed to his head and he bit his lip to keep from smiling. That was exactly the reason. "Do you need more wood?" he asked.

"I'm fine. And look, there she comes up the trail now. Get along; I'll finish the chores. Gather much raftal with the young lady. Perhaps you can convince the queen you're worth more than just magic. Maybe they'll honor you the same way they honor Constance."

Abbott raced to the door when he saw Constance through the window, but before he stepped outside, he turned to Claudia. "Don't worry, Mum. Everything will turn out happily. The queen won't kill me. I promise."

"Are you ready to hike?" Constance called.

"Go on. Have fun. Enjoy the sunshine." Claudia shuffled him out the door.

Abbott eagerly jumped down the porch and smiled at Constance, and then his shoulders dropped. "You changed your clothes! You're dressed like a warrior woman." The taupe balloon pants, the green tunic and knife tucked in her belt reminded him of Deanna and the other guards who kept him prisoner.

"I can't go walking in the woods in a dress! Why does it matter to you?"

"It doesn't, I guess. I just thought that maybe for a little while, I wouldn't have to think about being a prisoner. I thought I could just have fun."

"I didn't know my clothes would bother you. You don't have to come with me, you know. But this is how I always dress when I'm in the woods."

"I'm sorry. Let's just have a good time."

"Let's make a deal. You forget about being a prisoner and I'll forget about being lonesome. How does that sound?"

"Good!"

Constance was just as tall as Abbott, so he didn't have to run to keep up with her like he had to with the warrior women, or Claudia. And seeing straight across to her eyes was a new sensation. Rarely did he ever get to look into someone's eyes without having to look up. And she had such pretty eyes too, a blue sky on a winter's day. Clear and shiny. Her cheeks were rosy and brightened when she smiled, which made him smile.

They walked quietly for a while.

"You're lonesome?"

"Always."

"Is it because there's no one your age in the castle?"

Constance shrugged. "That's part of it. It's also because I'm odd to them. I'm not a Taikan, you know."

"I didn't think so. Neither am I."

She laughed. "I know that."

She grabbed his hand and pulled him off the trail. "Come this way. The guards keep watch around that bend, and they mustn't see us together."

Abbott ran alongside of her when he could when the bramble wasn't in the way. He stumbled over rocks and bumped into spider webs. Sticks scratched his arms and thorns caught his hair. Constance moved gracefully, dodging branches, and jumping over obstacles. She ran ahead of him to a clearing and waited. The trees here were larger than any trees Abbott had ever seen. Enormous trunks twice the size of his own body surrounded him, their roots wound and twisted under and over the ground. Lichen hung to their branches like beards on old men and green moss covered their bark.

"We're safe now." Constance said. "They never come into this part of the woods. They think they are haunted."

"Are they?"

Constance shrugged and petted the soft moss on one exceptionally large tree trunk. "Maybe they are the wizards Hacatine killed because they seem so old and wise. I'm glad her warriors are afraid to come here."

He panted and welcomed the rest, brushing the dirt from his hair. "Where are we going?"

"You'll see. It's not too far and we don't have to run anymore." She led him deeper into them. Abbott had to bend backwards to see the top if the woods. The firs stood apart from one another, giving Abbott and Constance ample room to walk side by side.

"What kind of magic do you have?" Constance broke the silence this time.

"I have my father's magic."

"What does it do?"

He laughed. "Not much. I see things, but not all the time. Only sometimes. I can see into people and read their past. Like I read an ocean voyage in yours."

"Oh." She frowned. "What else did you read about me?"

Abbott shrugged. "That things were hard for you, too."

"It's over now. I enjoy it here. They're good enough for me and I can get over my loneliness, especially now that I have a friend." She smiled at him and when she did, it sent a tickling sensation through him.

"Do you want to tell me about where you come from?" His voice softened.

She stopped, crossed her arms and leaned against a tree. "Why? You can find out on your own. Just look." She opened her eyes wide.

He laughed. "I'd rather you told me. I see things, but I don't always know what they mean. Besides, I only want to know what you want to tell me."

"Well, I don't remember much. I remember getting seasick. And what about you? How did you get to be a prisoner?"

"They kidnapped me. I was fishing with my uncle, and when we went to get a net, they grabbed me. Two of the warrior women."

A pout returned to her face. "I'm sorry. The queen has ugly plans for you, doesn't she?"

Abbott looked away. "I don't care what her plans are. She will not carry them out. I'll be long gone before then."

"Either way will break my heart."

Abbott studied her eyes. She meant it.

Constance took his hand. "Come on. Let's just have fun today. Look. Mushrooms! I love mushrooms."

"So do I!" There was no reason to stay somber. The sun was out, the woods were majestic, and Constance was beautiful.

"I love to walk in the woods," Constance said.

"I always walked in the forest back home. Sometimes we would go to the salmon creek. I miss my home."

"I feel sorry for you."

When they came to a log covered with moss, Constance sat down. "It's soft!" she said, nodding for him to sit next to her.

"You're tired?".

She shook her head and then touched her lips with her finger. "This is the harvest place. But you must be quiet."

He gave her a questioning look. She patted the log again and he sat next to her.

"Just sit quietly for a moment. You'll see why we're here."

Abbott sighed, and then relaxed, watching the golden leaves of autumn play with the sunlight that trickled through the forest. Constance sat as still as the log they rested on, her arms folded across her chest, her head held high, and a slight smile on her face. His gaze settled on the silky white hair that fell over her shoulders, curly in some parts, where it met her tunic, and then loose waves as it fell over her back. He wondered about the color. Only old men and women had white hair, but not nearly as shiny and soft as hers. Strands of copper hue wove through her curls. His staring must have been intrusive, for she looked at him once and the contact sent a chill down his spine. The moment was so intimate he could have known her all his life.

"What are we waiting for?" he asked.

"That!" Constance nodded toward the brush nearby.

"I don't see anything."

"That's because you're not looking. On the fern, next to the old stump, look closely. Look for something yellow."

Abbott squinted and searched and finally caught sight of a butterfly.

"Wait here." She moved cautiously toward the creature that now rested on a fern. She sang the same melody Abbott had heard her sing in the castle. When she reached out, the yellow wings opened, and the creature flitted and then landed on her hand. As she stood perfectly motionless, the butterfly at the tip of her fingers secreted a white substance which resembled a stream of the whipped milk Rosalind used to give him. The butterfly rose into the air several times, shooting its slender legs as it created its silk onto the pile that grew higher and higher in her palm. Once Constance's hand was filled, the butterfly flew away.

Abbott sighed and laughed, not realizing he had been holding his breath. But before he could say anything, Constance put the substance into her mouth, and with both hands and fingers moving as quick as the butterfly's legs had, she gently pulled a string of thread through the space between her teeth, spinning rapidly as it came out. She sat on the log next to Abbott again. When her task was complete, a neat pile of thread lay on her lap. She grinned at Abbott, who was lost for words.

"I can teach you to do this, too. We could come here together every afternoon and gather raftal. It would be a way for us to forget our troubles. It would be something that you and I could share in secret.

"I'm not sure I could do that," he nodded toward her lap, showing the thread. "But I could try. If nothing else, I would come and watch you."

Constance tucked the thread in the pocket of in her pants and stood. "There are other things I do in the forest, too. I collect herbs."

"What herbs?"

"Promise you won't tell?"

Abbott nodded, and she leaned over to whisper in his ear. Her breath was sweet smelling, and it tickled his neck, but he held back his laugh. "Dragon leaf."

"I've never heard of it."

"It's native to Taikus and only grows in these forests. Look, there's some right there!" Constance tied the raftal around her belt and drew her knife, sliding off the log. With one slice, she had a stalk in her hand and brought it to him. "See the four-pointed leaves on the stem?"

He nodded.

"Only Dragon Leaf has ridges along the edge. Like a dragon's scale."

"Why do you gather Dragon leaf?"

"It has healing properties." She harvested another stalk, tucked the knife back in her belt, and returned to his side.

"And why do you need a healing herb?" Abbott was familiar with healing plants, which his mother used to harvest on the Isle of Refuge. The gypsies gathered them occasionally too, but only when someone was hurt or sick. "Is something wrong with you?"

She shook her head. "No. Not me. But…" She squinted at him and leaned away. "Can I trust you?"

"Why do you ask that? Didn't you just trust me with your secret raftal spinning? There aren't many people on this island I would tell a secret to." Abbott thought for a moment. "The only person who is kind to me is Claudia. I might confide in her, but not if you don't want me to."

"Well, Claudia already knows about this."

"What?"

"There are caves here on Taikus. A labyrinth of tunnels and channels. Lots of people get lost in there. None of Hacatine's warriors like to go there."

"Oh! That sounds like a hideout!" Abbott liked the idea; certain he'd be able to navigate through caves. He was a good explorer.

"It is a refuge for the wizards who were imprisoned years ago, and who were stripped of their powers."

Abbott sensed the urgency of Constance's confession. "They didn't die like everyone says they did?"

She shook her head. "Not all of them. Some of them are still very sick. It takes a long time for a wizard or sorceress to recover from being stripped of their powers."

"So Hacatine's enemies aren't dead, like she thinks they are?"

Constance nodded, wide eyed.

"Who is hiding them? How did they get to the caves?"

"The humans took them there. Anglers, boat builders, farmers, and shepherds. They found the wizards outside the city left for dead, drained of energy with damaged hearts, although some of them went crazy. The healers started using Dragon's Leaf and saw what wonderful things the herb does. When they found that there was still hope, the commoners started rescuing the wizards, and one by one, secretly took them away to the caves. There are wizards who have fully recovered and are helping others to heal. Even though they don't get their magical powers back, still, at least they have life."

"They live in the caves?"

She nodded.

"And Claudia knows about this?"

Constance put her finger to her lips. "Please don't tell anyone."

"I'm a wizard. I'm in just as much danger as everyone else. Why would I tell?"

"I wanted you to know because I wanted to give you hope."

Abbott scowled. "She will not hurt me. I will not let her."

"She wants to. Maybe you can escape and live there in the caves someday."

"I have plans ongoing home. Still, I'd like to know where these caves are. I could go there and from the caves, go home."

"Not today. If you disappeared, Hacatine would have her warriors searching everywhere for you and then she might find everyone else too if you'hide in the caves. But you could help them."

"How?"

"You have magic, don't you?"

"Yes. A little. But what good would my magic do?"

"You could use it on the wizards. We think maybe magic, and Dragon's Leaf, might help their powers to return."

"Their magic, you mean?"

"Maybe."

"I could try. My father told me I was born in a cave," Abbott whispered. "I wonder if it's the same place."

"There aren't many caves in Taikus."

"Can we go there now?"

Constance glanced at the afternoon sky. "No. I told you. I have to be home by supper."

"How far is it from here?"

"About as far as we've already come."

"What will they do to you if you're late for supper?"

She jumped up too suddenly, and too cheerfully. "Never mind that. It doesn't matter. Let's go!"

GLOOM

They raced through the woods, hopping over roots and dodging the brush that protruded over their path. The trail took them into marsh and wetlands before a sharp incline slowed them down. Abbott panted as he caught up to Constance and plucked a leaf from out of her pure white hair.

She looked over her shoulder when she spoke. "It's not much farther. But we must be careful now. Warrior women are often found hunting in these parts because the deer come down from the highlands to graze in the meadow. If they saw us here, we'd be in trouble. But worse, no one's supposed to know where the entrance to the cave is."

Abbott dared not speak. The last thing he wanted was to get in trouble again, if for no other reason than for Claudia's sake. Constance stopped to bundle her hair in a bun and tuck it in her collar. She pulled out a green hood and pulled it over her head. With her knife drawn, she crouched low and walked cautiously. Abbott followed suit, though the boots he wore were clumsy and noisy. At the edge of the forest, they looked out over the meadow where a doe and fawn grazed peacefully. Beyond the grassland was a stone cliff.

"That's it?" Abbott asked. Black rock stretched to the graying sky. Rain clouds hinted at a coming storm.

"Yes," Constance answered.

"How do you get there without stepping out into the open?"

"You don't. But you don't have to stand out like a red flag on a ship's mast either. Do what I do. Crawl!"

No sooner did their bellies hit the ground than the doe lifted her head and froze. Abbott wished they hadn't spooked her. It would be safer for them if they had gone unnoticed in case someone else was lurking in the woods. Constance kept moving, unchanged by the startled deer. No warriors appeared, and the doe and her fawn simply wandered farther away.

Abbott slid along the grass behind Constance. When they came to the other side of the meadow, they stayed in the shadow of the cliffs up against the cold rocks. She led him directly to a tiny crack between two boulders. "This is the mouth of the cave," she whispered.

"That?"

She nodded, sucked in her breath in and slid through the crevice. Abbott squeezed in after her. "Makes me wonder how wizards even know about this place! Did they use magic to get in?"

There was no light inside. As soon as the rock walls surrounded him, damp musty fragrance permeated the air. At first it smelled sweet, like mushrooms and mint. But as Abbott felt his way through the tunnel, the sweetness subsided. He kept his hands on the rock walls and stayed as near to Constance as he could. He wasn't afraid. But his heart pounded uneasily against his ribs. Maybe they shouldn't have come so far, so late in the day. If there is a storm brewing, he and Constance might have difficulty going home.

"Do you still have your raftal?" he asked, wiping the cool sweat from his brow.

She stopped. "Yes. Why?"

"Because if we're late, it will be good for you to at least have an offering for the queen."

She laughed with a snicker disguised in her breath. "We'll only be here a bit. I just want them to see you. I want them to know you're here."

One more corner and they came to a cavern that was lit by candlelight. Met by a man who pivoted around in surprise, Constance jumped back into Abbott, knocking him off balance. Abbott caught himself from falling by reaching out for the wall.

"Dante, I'm sorry. I forgot the signal," she said.

"You need to stop sneaking up on us. You could get killed."

Dante was afraid in his eyes. Not much more than a skeleton. The man's flesh pulled tight against his high cheekbones. Light from the torches danced a deathly look across his face. "Who's that?" Dante fixed his stare on Abbott, sending a shiver down the boy's spine.

"This is Abbott. He's a prisoner of Hacatine's."

"Why did you bring him here?"

"He's a wizard."

The smell of burning wax mixed with other putrid odors caused Abbott to gag. Groans and distant cries of agony pulled his attention to the mouth of the cavern where bodies lie on sheepskins. One other person stooped among them, wiping a patient's head with a damp cloth.

"Has he come to help us?" Dante interrupted Abbott's thoughts as the man pressed Constance for an answer. He leaned over and glared at him with bloodshot eyes. So near was he Abbott could smell his rotting teeth.

"If I can." Abbott swallowed. It was then Abbott looked into Dante's past, not meaning to go so far. The torture in the man's soul bound Abbott, pulling him in like a magnet. There was no happiness that Abbott could see, only dread. Pain was the root of all that Dante was. Abbott stepped back and looked away, holding his breath to control his rapid pulse. "But I'm not sure what I can do for you."

"If you don't save us, you'll become one of us." The man straightened into his lanky stand and gestured to the mouth of the cavern. "They're dying."

Abbott kept his gaze on Constance. Somehow, her beauty quieted the sick feeling that gushed through his stomach. "I can help gather Dragon's Leaf."

"We need more than that, son. We need magic."

"Abbott needs time to come up with a plan, I think. Let us come back." Constance took Abbott's hand and tugged him toward the tunnel.

Dante moved away. "A plan. Yeah. Come back with a plan or our race will be annihilated forever. We need young people like you with a fresh look, a fresh life. A wizard's youth."

Abbott took one last look at Dante. The hunger in the man's soul was not only for food but also for a way out of his torturous plight. As frightening as he looked, Dante was one of Abbott's kind. A wizard bound to the fate of Abbott's father.

"There's got to be a way to help everyone," Abbott whispered.

When he felt Constance pulling him back into the tunnel again, he followed. But the sight of Dante, and that cave, burned an image in his mind he couldn't release.

They hurried. It was a good thing Constance knew her way out, for with all the little side burrows and junctions, if he were alone, he'd be completely lost. Abbott hadn't realized how sick the sight and smell of those men made him until he was well into the tunnels. But he braved through the churning stomach and was grateful when he could taste the coolness and fresh air outside, now wet with a steady mist.

Abbott shivered. His tunic absorbed the damp as soon as he stepped into the rain, and when he lowered his body close to the ground to cross the meadow, mud clung to his knees and caked on his boots. Constance slipped along ahead of him. Her hood bounced in rhythm to the graceful movement of her body. When they slithered through the wet grass of the meadow and came to the forest edge, she stopped and waited for him. Her face was covered with mud, her hair stringy and wet, drips of rain trickled down her cheeks.

"You're a mess," she said to Abbott.

He laughed. "So are you."

A sudden clap of thunder startled him. Lightning bolted across the clouds. Neither Abbott nor Constance had to prod the other to move. They heard pouring rain come from the west and ran into the forest hoping the trees would umbrella the violence of the downpour, but there was no escape from the storm. Within minutes, they were drenched. Mud hindered their speed. Constance slipped and fell, and Abbott helped her up. Too dangerous to hurry, they walked. The forest became dark, the shadows heavy, Abbott couldn't tell if it was merely the cloud cover that shadowed them, or if night was approaching.

"Do you still have that ball of thread?" Abbott asked.

Constance lifted the raftal that hung wet and muddy on her belt. "Look at it," she wiped her nose with her sleeve.

"You can wash it, can't you?"

"It's a mess and I'll get in trouble for bringing it home in this condition. I'd be better off if I didn't even have it."

"Why?"

"Well, because once it's like this, it isn't worthy of the queen, that's why. Here!" She handed it to Abbott.

"You want me to take it? What will you tell them you've been doing all day?"

"I'll tell them I couldn't gather raftal because of the rain. Take it home with you. Claudia will keep it safe and then maybe I can come over and do something for you with it. I can't bring raftal looking like this into the castle. And I can't throw it away. To do so would be disrespectful to the butterfly. I suppose this gift is yours." She pushed it toward him. "Here! Take it."

Abbott took the ball of yarn and tucked it into his pocket.

"Let's go, Abbott! I must be home before dark."

"You won't be. It's already dark."

The sun had set. Night brought the wind, more lightning and thunder that rattled the earth under their feet. What should have been a straight path home turned into trails he hadn't remembered passing. Constance was lost, and he did not know how to get home either. When they emerged from the forest edge, they ended up at the beach, and not in the village.

"At least we can find our way home now." Abbott looked up the hill toward Hacatine's castle. Clouds flew across the sky behind the fortress.

"I guess we should go our own way now." Constance turned to him. She pulled the hood off her head and pushed her wet hair out of her eyes. "I hope you aren't in too much trouble."

"You, too." Abbott could see the fear she felt right now, even though she was trying to hide it. If only he could see her future and not just her past and present, he would know if she was in danger. But that was a skill he had very little experience with. "Maybe you should just come home with me?"

She shook her head and laughed. "No. That would be crazy. They would know. The queen would be outraged."

"Claudia knows I'm with you. Did you tell the people in the castle who you were going to be with?"

Constance shrugged. "That would've been stupid. I'm better off being alone than being with a prisoner."

Abbott looked away.

"I didn't mean it like that. It's just that's how the warrior women would look at it."

"Have you ever been out after dark before?" he asked.

She shook her head. "I'll tell them I got lost. Which I did so I won't be lying to them."

"I'll walk you to the castle. As far as the lion."

She might have argued, but Abbott went ahead of her.

END OF CHILDHOOD

When Constance disappeared through the palace doors, Abbott was left with an empty and sick feeling. He walked home alone, thinking about her, about raftal, and butterflies, and wizards cringing in a cold and dismal cave. She was so pretty, and the cave was so dark. What a strange day, and disturbing world. He stomped the mud off his boots before he went inside Claudia's house. There were no words to give the woman when he shut the door behind him. He had no excuses.

"Did Constance make it home all right?"

"Yes," Abbott sat on the floor by the door and pulled his boots off, shaking the dirt from inside of them.

"It's late, you know."

"I know."

Claudia cleared her throat. "She'll be punished."

"I'm sorry." He blinked back tears, regretting the trouble they were in. Sorry wasn't enough to express how he felt. "We didn't mean to be gone so long, honest." After he pulled his tunic over his head, he hung it on a chair by the fire to dry. "She took me to see the wizards."

"That explains why you're so late. Say nothing to anyone about what you saw."

"I won't. What will they do to her?"

"I don't know. It depends on what she tells them." Claudia rose, pulled a towel from the table, and motioned him to stand. When he did, she dropped the towel on his head and dried his hair vigorously. "You could get sick traipsing through the woods dressed as you were in that weather."

"It was a horrible place."

"The caves? Yes. I know."

"You've been there?"

"Once or twice."

He watched Claudia hang the towel next to his tunic on a chair. She put a log on the fire and poked at the embers until the flames jumped up the chimney. The house filled with warmth and the sweet smell of burning cedar.

"She spun raftal for me," Abbot walked to the chair and pulled the wet yarn from the pocket.

"She gave raftal to you?"

"She said it was too spoiled to bring into the castle.

Claudia took the yarn from him, inspecting it as she unraveled the string. "Let's dry it by the fire. This is a precious gift you have here, Abbott. There are few creatures like her in this world. Think pleasantly about her. Perhaps the queen won't be too harsh."

"I can't help but think good things about Constance. It was fun today. That is until we went to the caves and saw all the sick men. And until we had to run home in the pouring rain, and it got dark and we got lost."

His eyes rested on the flames in the fireplace. "She wants me to save the wizards. I'm going to, you know."

"Perhaps. It 'd make sense. Maybe that's why Providence has you here. You might also need to save your little friend, Constance, too."

"I wish I could do it now. But I'm just a child."

"You will be a man in a few years." Claudia's words cut to his heart.

"That's not what everyone is saying." He glanced at her, wondering what kind of reaction his words would prompt. "Everyone is telling me I'm going to die when I'm eighteen. That's not being a man. That's not growing up."

"And you believe everyone?"

He shrugged.

"Believe in yourself, Abbott. Your father faced the same fate you're facing, and he's still alive, well past the age of eighteen, I might add. The men in the caves, they're alive. Maybe my son is still alive. Hacatine will not kill you if you decide not to let her."

Abbott listened, absorbing her words. "The warrior women need to be saved, too."

Claudia laughed as she took a seat by the fire and covered herself with a blanket. "That may not be possible."

"Why not? They're good. Justine is kind when she's not doing what the queen tells her to. And Deanna saw all her family die except her mother, who was still crying for her to come home. Who knows the story of the others?"

Startled, Claudia looked at him. "You used your magic on Deanna?"

"Just that one time. I would do it again. Everyone here is troubled, and someone needs to see it. They're all hiding from each other. They need a leader."

"And you're their leader?"

Abbott straightened. "Why wait until I'm grown? Why wait until I'm sick and must drink Dragon's Leaf in a dark and creepy cave? Why not now?"

He waited for her to answer his questions, but Claudia just sat there staring at the fire, rocking occasionally. Abbott sat next to her and focused on the flames as she tucked the blanket over him. The silence helped him settle his thoughts.

"Have a plan," she finally whispered. "You must reflect on all things. Don't rush."

"Will you help me?"

"I'll do what I can."

The next spring

Rain kept Abbott indoors. Clouds grew in intensity, lightning flashed, and balls of ice fell from the sky. After hail came snow. The colder the weather, the less Abbott wandered away from Claudia's house. On a gray and stormy day, a messenger came to their door from the palace. A warrior woman bundled in furs, boots up to her knees and packed with snow, knocked on the door. Her hair tucked into a cap, her cheeks were rosy, and when she talked her words came out with a cloud of steam.

"Word from the palace," she said, and handed a parchment rolled and sealed with wax, which Claudia took immediately.

"Thank you." Claudia said.

The woman walked away, her tracks soon covered by falling snow. When Claudia shut the door, she broke the seal and unrolled the scroll.

"Look here, Abbott. We have orders from the queen." Her blue eyes rested on his.

It's not good news either, is it?" he asked. She shook her head.

"Neither you nor I can return to the castle unless we're summonsed."

"That's our punishment? I can't see Constance anymore?"

Abbott's shoulders sank. He walked to the bench and stared at the flames that were always in the fireplace, always alive, always dancing bright orange and gold. Always giving heat whenever Claudia feeds it. But being warm by only a fire was lonely. He missed the turquoise sky, the forest, and his friend.

"Do you think Constance is confined to the castle?"

"She may very well be."

"What about Raftal? How will Constance spin in the cold weather? How will the queen get her clothes now?"

"Don't brood, Abbott. We don't know what's happening. Let's make that soup we started." Claudia set her shawl on the hook, glanced at him and nodded toward the kitchen. "You can cut the carrots."

He followed her to the kitchen, rolled up his sleeves and washed his hands.

"Raftal is only harvested when it's warm," Claudia peeled the roots they had brought in from the cellar as she talked. "That's the only time the butterflies fly about. Look outside, Abbott. It's snowing. Are there any butterflies out there now?"

Abbott looked at the giant flakes of white crystals stuck to the window and sighed. "No, Mum. I don't see any."

"Hacatine has plenty of clothes to wear until springtime." Claudia scooped the vegetables into her hand, dropped them in the kettle and set the pot on the fire. "Constance would have stopped coming to the woods in the winter, anyway."

"I don't think she would have stopped coming to see me, though."

"Probably not." Claudia wiped her hands on her apron and ruffled his hair. "She likes you. Being separated from you won't change how she feels about you. If nothing else, it will make her like you more."

"Do you think I'll ever see her again?"

Claudia nodded. Abbott followed her as she carried the pot to the fireplace and set it on the coals. "Nothing is forever. Some days, I wonder if I'll ever see Silvio again. I still cling to the hope that I will. Especially now that I know your father is still alive. Cling to the hope that you will see Constance again."

"Do you think I'll see my father again, too?"

Though her thin lips curled into a smile, her nod was nothing more than a slight tremor. Her yes was not convincing.

Abbott wiped his hands on a towel and sat on the wooden bench in front of the fireplace. "That's what I'll do then. I'm going to hope I will see Constance again. I'm going to hope that you see your son again too. I hope everything comes out the way we want it to."

Claudia wiped the tear from her cheek. "Me too," she said.

***

Abbott hung onto those thoughts, but as the days grew into seasons, and winter passed into windy springs, hope faded. Summer came and went, and more winters crawled by. Still, Constance never showed her face in the forest, and he could not venture up the castle stairs. Abbott grew in stature as he changed from a boy into a young man, taking a fondness to the outdoors. He went fishing whenever he had a chance, trading his catch for commodities that Claudia needed, and giving the rest to the needy. His generosity impressed the villagers and common people. But his heart was bent on freeing the warrior women, and Constance if she were still alive. That's why, when he became a merchant in the queen's court, he welcomed the opportunity.

"It's an enormous responsibility, Abbott." Claudia shook her head in doubt.

"Yes. And it'll be mine!"

"You're so young still."

"I'm sixteen. That's old enough to man a table every day and to count coins. It will be good for me. Besides, I'll be introduced to many of the queen's servants in the marketplace."

"Ah. You have a secret agenda, do you? Every day you will have to trade at your table. You'll have to catch your fish in the evenings to bring to market the next morning. It will be a lot of work. And I'll still need you to bring me firewood."

Abbott laughed. "I will not abandon you, Mum. I'm doing this to help you. Think of all the things I can trade for and bring home to make your life easier! You won't have to feel like a prisoner ever again."

Times had changed, indeed. Ever since Claudia had been told not to return to the palace, their life had taken a turn for the better. No longer did they have to answer to the wicked queen, succumbing to her insults and petty punishments. Though Abbott lost access to his childhood friend, he and Claudia had gained a new life.

On the first day of the market, in the spring of his sixteenth year, with other village children assisting him, Abbott brought his fish to the courtyard in baskets. He arrived well before sunup and built a lean-to from reeds and bamboo he had harvested the day before and which would keep the scorching sun from spoiling his fish. The display was so attractively arranged that by dawn sorceresses and servants mingled under his roof. They selected choice fish and herbs from his booth and already he gained a pretty penny for his wares. When Abbott recognized Deanna and Justine walking through the busy streets of the market square, he called out to them.

"Justine! Deanna! Over here!" He waved.

"Abbott? Is that you? The little wizard?" Deanna squinted and neared.

"I'd hardly call him little anymore." Justine hurried to his table, a broad grin on her face. "You've grown so tall and handsome. It's good to see you! And you've found yourself a trade. You've adapted to Taikan lifestyle well!"

"I have." Abbott bowed in respect and gestured to his products. "What's your choice, ladies? Freshwater fillet, or the apple of the sea? And I want to give you a gift, Deanna." He held up one of his prize fish. "

"Me? Why me?" Deanna blushed.

"You were always a favorite of mine!" He smiled. His dark eyes twinkled as he caught her gaze. Perhaps if he saw into Deanna, he'd find out what happened to Constance.

"You have the wrong warrior. I was always your enemy."

"I never thought of you as an enemy."

She looked into his eyes and then tried pulling away, but Abbott was older now, his magic stronger. He held her until he found Constance in her memory, still spinning raftal in the castle, now a young woman.

"She's beautiful," he said under his breath. "She's still alive! Where is she?" he asked her, mesmerized by the vision in Deanna's mind.

"Where you first saw her," Deanna shuffled about nervously until Abbott released the hold he had on her. "Constance's talents have increased with her beauty. The cloth she weaves now has remarkable patterns that impress even the queen."

"Tell her I want to see her."

"I'll tell her, but rarely does the queen allow her any freedom anymore. Even when she gathers raftal, guards go with her and stand over her."

"Guards? That's ludicrous. She's not committed any crime. Why? Because when she was a child, she met a young friend in the woods. How can such a sentence be justified?"

Deanna shrugged; an eyebrow raised. "She was never supposed to have wandered. She works for the queen, Abbott. I'm certain even if she wanted to see you, she wouldn't be able to get away, especially not to meet with you. You forget you have limited freedom yourself. It's only a matter or time before you'll appear in Hacatine's court again, you know."

Abbott turned from her gaze and filled a basket for Deanna. "Then let Constance know I haven't forgotten about her." He handed her a sachet of herbs. Bring this to her as my gift. Tell her…" He hesitated. It was doubtful Deanna could deliver his message the way he would if he ever saw her again. "Tell her I think about her every day, and at night…" His eyes met Deanna's again. "At night, she is in my dreams." He smiled. That was perhaps too much for Deanna to relay. "And this is my gift to you." He held his offering out and when she reached to take it, he drew nearer.

"Someday you'll see your mother again and your life will be happy. Hold on to that hope. That day is not too far away."

Her face reddened. She took the basket and stepped back.

"And for you." Abbott handed Justine a basket. "A taste of both the sea and the river."

"You're not using your magic on me?"

"Do you want me to?"

"Only if it helps you to find an answer to our plight, Abbott the Wizard," she whispered.

That was exactly what he wanted to hear. If there was one warrior woman seeking freedom, then there were a hundred.

"If you have hunger, I have a feast." His voice was low. "We should meet. Bring your friends, the ones that think as you do."

"Thank you," she said as she took his offering. "When?"

"This evening on the beach. That would be a safe place, wouldn't it? There's an aspen grove near shore. I'll meet you there."

"At twilight?"

"At twilight."

Both Justine and Deanna walked away, leaving Abbott with more hope than he had had in a very long time.

RENDEZVOUS

Despite the danger, not once did Abbott regret making this engagement, though he wouldn't blame Justine if she chose not to come. It was riskier for a warrior woman to meet a prisoner in secret than it was for him. Still, the queen's servants had more to gain from escaping Hacatine's tyranny than anyone else.

Abbott sat on the driftwood under the aspens, the beach, and the castle stairway in full view. If someone approached from the city, he'd be able to see them. Several fishers had passed by earlier that day. They gathered their nets from the beach and launched their gigs. The beach knew no other visitors that afternoon.

Tide crept away, leaving a dark layer of sand, wet rock and seagulls fighting over clams. The louder the birds squawked; the more other gulls hovered over them. Abbott laughed at the birds but jumped at the sound of a twig snapping in the woods and a body so near, he felt her breath.

"You're startled?"

"You caught me off guard," he answered.

"You didn't expect us to walk boldly down the palace stairs, did you?"

Abbott turned and laughed nervously when he saw it was Justine. "I didn't know what to expect!" He stood to face her, surprised no one was at her side. "You came alone?"

"No!" Her answer was quick and her voice quiet. "There are others. However, they're not very trusting of wizards."

Abbott exhaled, confused. He had done nothing to hurt anyone.

Justine explained. "For all the pain and sorrow that Hacatine has caused the wizards, we fear retaliation. I had to convince them you're on our side." When Abbott lifted his brow, she added, "Rather you're on the side we would be on if we weren't Hacatine's warriors."

"And they're convinced?"

"I think so, but you might have to confirm your sincerity."

"And how would I do that?"

She smiled. "I'm sure you'll think of something. Follow me."

She led him through low brush and hanging branches farther into the thicket until woods surrounded them and the beach and castle were far from view. Gold from the last rays of the day's sun glistened on the treetops above his head, casting a glow on the faces of the women he approached. Three of the women lingered in a clearing. Three sat on a fallen log, the other two stood nearby, and one held a bow with an arrow nocked and aimed at Abbott. He stopped and raised his hands.

"No need for that, Rosa!" Justine said to the archer. "He's come in peace."

Rosa lowered her weapon but did not release the tension. Abbott did not lower his hands. Justine stepped in between the two. "This is Abbott. He's willing to hear our grievances and help us."

"Justine, how can a wizard help us?" The woman jumped up from the log, swinging her flaming red hair behind her shoulders. She scrutinized Abbott and then addressed Justine. "I don't understand how we can start a rebellion led by a prisoner barely older than a boy! None of us possess any kind of power stronger than the queen's. Not even a wizard can match her sorcery. It'll be a foolish move."

"Frambella, sit down and let's hear the man out. Maybe he has some sort of trickery up his sleeve, some devious plan we've not thought of." A heavier, lighter skin woman tugged at Frambella's hand, beckoning her to sit. The woman on the fallen log made eye contact with Abbott and then looked away.

"I've yet to succumb to a wizard, Justine." A voice came from the shadow of an aspen. "We're doing fine without him. He's dead meat for Hacatine. Why should we risk our necks for him? Chances are, he'll free himself and leave us to the queen's dogs."

"Madam!" Abbott balked at the woman's words. The warrior leaning against the tree raised her brow in surprise. "If I wanted to save my skin, I would do so without risking yours. I can think of several ways to leave this island. I would be much safer going alone."

"Then why are you here?" Frambella pushed her tongue against the inside of her cheek. "Why don't you just make a run for it? We all know what fate awaits you. Why do you linger?"

"I have interests here."

"Ha!" Frambella looked at the others, as though to lead a chorus of mockery, but no one joined her.

"What interests?" the dark one in the shadows asked.

"Claudia, for one. She's been a mother to me. I can't leave her alone to Hacatine's torture. And there are others I've promised to help escape. Less able bodied, ill and needy. And…" Abbott wasn't sure he should talk about Constance, but his heart ached for her. "And there is one who lives in the confines of the castle who deserves freedom and has less than you or I."

Perhaps his plea was better received than he expected. Silence was the response.

"He has a heart," someone finally whispered from the shadows.

Abbott sighed. "Ever since I was young, the plight of the Taikans has moved me. I feel for all of you."

Frambella tossed her hair again and sat down. Abbott followed her with his eyes. "Do you discount what I say? You think I'm not sincere?"

"I think you lie like all the other men on the island."

Abbot kneeled in front of her. "Look at me."

When their eyes met, the image in her memory shocked him. Her past was as vivid as the forest they stood in. "Hacatine took your child?" he whispered gently. "A boy?"

Frambella looked away without answering.

"Your son was a wizard, wasn't he?" Since the day Abbott arrived in Taikus he'd not seen a single wizard save for the renegades in the caves. A sorceress would give birth to a magic child. And who was its father? Abbott pressed to make eye contact again. "What did the queen do with him?" His heart raced, afraid of the answer yet desperate to find out. "She didn't kill him, did she?"

"Hacatine keeps the children under guard. Few know where they're being raised, but we know they're alive." Justine interrupted. "Don't torture her so, Abbott. She still grieves."

Abbott caught his breath and slowly rose to his feet, touching Frambella gently on her shoulder. "I'm sorry for your pain."

The sorceress brushed his hand away.

"We can free them." He looked at the others, who showed no urgency in their posture.

"You're so young and foolish. Do you honestly think freeing the children isn't in our hearts?" The shadow woman snickered and stepped into the fading daylight. Taller than Abbott, her hair was black as coal, her eyes umber and filled with spark. "You don't understand the power of your enemy. Hacatine has taken our gifts and absorbed them into her own magic. She can read our minds, so we dare not think rebellion when she's nearby. There's nothing that can kill her. She's never given birth, and yet she knows those of us who have will die. She uses it against us. Frambella is a slave to her because of that, and because of that, we all fear loving a man. Every warrior woman who tends to the offspring is under a spell and will kill on sight. You can't break it, Abbott. You can't break her."

"Rhonda, he has hope. Don't destroy it," Justine interrupted.

"Ah! Hope, yes! The dying hope of a Wayward, and in love with one too, I might add."

Stunned, Abbott steadied his gaze on the woman.

"That's right, wizard. I can see your heart. It's the gift Hacatine let me keep."

He broke contact with Rhonda as a bead of sweat trickled past his cheek. "If you don't have hope, what do you have?"

"Death. Many of us go about life as though dead. Can you fight death, wizard boy?"

"I've never tried," he muttered under his breath. Rhonda returned to the shadows and as she did, he raised his head. "But there's life in you and if we fight and lose, then we die. But if we fight and win, we'll be able to live that life to its fullest. What's losing, then?"

"I'm with you, Abbott." Justine stepped to his side and offered her hand. "That's what we're here for."

Though they touched for only a second, he felt the heat of her magic.

Justine spoke to the woman seated. "Viola? Are you with us?"

"Do we have a choice? We either continue aiding Hacatine, or we resist. She's destroyed our island and our lives, and now she aims to destroy the Northland and the winds. I'm tired of fighting, but if we don't stand against her, I fear I'll be fighting for the rest of my life against enemies I would otherwise consider friends."

The air chilled as daylight slipped into night and the first star of the evening appeared through the treetops.

Abbott waited for someone else to speak, and when no one did, he cleared his throat. "Three people? That's it? Maybe we should forget this meeting and go home as though words between us were never spoken."

Again silence.

"Where is Deanna?" Abbott asked quietly.

"Deanna didn't come. She cautioned against meeting you here tonight." Rhonda's harsh voice cut like a sword. "She never had a heart for wizards and called us fools. I think she's right."

"Let's go." It was Rosa who nodded toward the other women. "There's nothing for us here."

All but Justine and Viola vanished through the woods; their steps quiet as deer.

Abbott collapsed on the ground and ran his fingers through his hair. "There has to be a way."

Viola's spoke softly. "We need a plan. What do you propose? None of the warrior women will join a rebellion without a plan."

"I can't come up with a plan if no one is behind it. What if you encouraged your friends a little at a time? Talk about what this island could be like if…"

"If what?" Viola interrupted. "If Hacatine were dead?"

Those were not his words and once they were spoken, they sounded unachievable.

"If Taikus were the way it used to be!" Justine interrupted. "If death to the queen is what will return peace to Taikus, then so be it."

"You cannot kill the woman, Justine. None of us can," Viola assured her.

"If," Abbott paused while collecting his thoughts. "If the queen were to leave the island for a time…"

The suggestion caught their attention.

"War would be the only reason Hacatine would leave Taikus."

"I see."

"And we would be required to sail alongside her. We would have no part in your plan."

"I need more time to think."

Viola nudged Justine. "Let's go."

The women turned to leave, taking Abbott's hope with them. He called softly before they came to the dark of the woods.

"Justine,"

She stopped and waited.

"If you can, without putting yourself in danger, would you please give word to Constance that I…" he hesitated. "Please tell her I wish to see her."

"She's been waiting to hear from you," Justine assured him.

REUNION

Abbott made a point of visiting the woods the next morning on his way to the fishing hole. Surely the queen wouldn't hold a grudge for eight years, not against someone who made silk only for her.

Melting snow chilled the air, the cold ground crunched under his feet, but tiny trilliums sprang from the frost. With his lance resting on his shoulder, he hiked through the budding aspens. Refreshed, and alive, a heartbeat of anticipation spurred him on until he came to the log where he and Constance sat years ago–the exact spot where he'd seen her spin raftal for the very first time. He rested, his eyes opened wide, watching her while he listened to the quiet sounds of the forest.

There were no footsteps, no sign that anyone approached, but in the sunlight a shadow fluttered by. The yellow wings of the monarch appeared. Without a sound, he moved toward the creature and, when he was near enough, he held out his hand. The butterfly flitted delicately across his skin. She stepped onto his finger, her touch barely noticeable, and then settled in his hand. He stood perfectly still, holding his breath as she circled and started spinning its silk. First, one thin thread appeared, which the butterfly gathered into a ball. The tickle of her little legs made Abbott smile, but the memory of Constance brought tears to his eyes. With a large ball of silk formed, the butterfly broke the thread and flew away.

"Now put it in your mouth."

Startled, Abbott looked up. The sun shone behind Constance, casting her silhouette amongst the ferns. No longer the little girl he once knew, he still recognized her.

"Go on. It tastes sweet, but don't swallow it!"

Abbott touched the silk to his lips and then placed the fragile ball of waxy thread on his tongue.

"Now close your teeth and grab a bit of the thread. Spin it in-between your thumb and your pointy finger."

Abbott did as he was told, though his fingers were much clumsier than he remembered hers being. He wanted to speak, but his mouth was full. She coached him through the process, though his thread came out thick and lumpy.

"Let me help. It can only last so long in your mouth before your body digests it. You must spin fast. Here."

Constance reached to his lips and took the silk with her slender fingers, spinning rapidly. He held his hands below hers to catch the ball of yarn. When the last of the silk had been spun, she leaned forward and, just as delicate as the butterfly that had stepped onto his finger, she touched his lips with hers.

"I missed you."

Abbott felt a fever rush through him, and his heart beat hard. He hadn't realized how much he missed her until now. "And I, you," he said.

"Let's run away together."

She'd grown. No longer the skinny white-haired little girl spinning in the queen's parlor, Constance had blossomed into a lovely young woman. Her braids caught the sun and glistened with speckles of copper. A kirtle of earthen brown draped over a linen smock accented her graceful figure. She teased him with a smile.

"You're serious?"

"As ever." Constance tightened the knot on her belt and looped the yarn over it. She tugged the leather binding with smooth hands.

"You were imprisoned for eight years because of me. If we failed, wouldn't you be risking a lifetime sentence?"

"I already have a lifetime sentence." She looked up at him. "But why would they find us?"

Abbott's heart beat hard. At that moment, the urge to touch her was overwhelming, yet he fought it. "Where would we go?"

"To the caves."

"And Claudia?" Living in a dark cave, always on the run, was not something he wanted for either of them. But then, what other fate did he have to look forward to? Life had been bright for him this year. Escape would bring a storm. He shook his head.

"Abbott, she's going to slay you. You've only two more years before she'll call for you."

"In two years, I will have pleased the entire court. There's a rebellion brewing. We can escape when we have an army."

She blushed as a grimace darkened her face. "The warrior women?"

"Yes."

Constance turned. Abbott took her arm and brought her back.

"Which one?" she asked.

"Which one what?"

"Which one do you love?"

"No! Don't think like that. None of them. I care for them, yes. They are tormented, and I should rescue them. But I'm not in love with any of them. It's you…" He didn't finish what his heart wanted him to say. He didn't know how.

"And you want to rescue me? That's it? You feel sorry for me?"

"Yes." Abbott spoke softly. She pushed his hands from her shoulders and stepped back. "That's all? You just want to help me, is all?"

"Well, yes, I want to help you but… but that's not all."

"What then?"

Her eyes grew wide and open. Her past seemed like a road map before him, and yet he refused to follow it. He wanted only to connect to her now. "Eight years ago, when you and I ran off together, something inside of me came alive. Even though we were young and playful, I felt a kinship with you." He took both her hands in his. "When Hacatine took you away from me, I never forgot. I have been torn from everything I knew–my family, my home. But nothing caused greater heartache than to be separated from you."

She drew nearer. He didn't want to see what lay beyond her tears. There would be a time for that. Someday he would know all that she's gone through. Not now. He refused to feel anger for her mistreatment, or pity for what she suffered. He looked away from the depth of her mind.

He wanted only to love her.

Their lips met. He wrapped his arms around her, and she caressed his neck as their bodies closed distance. How soft she was, how warm, as she pressed up against him. Her heart fluttered against his chest. He had never in his life experienced such ecstasy.

Swiftly to the Hills

"Come, mother," Abbott rushed into Claudia's house, collecting blankets, coats and whatever else he found important, packing the items into a duffle bag which Constance held open for him.

Claudia emerged from the kitchen; her face paled from the shock of his urgency.

"Abbott, what are you doing? Did things not go well at the market today?"

He looked up at her briefly and wiped his hair out of his eyes. "We're leaving. Now!"

"Abbott," Claudia protested.

"Don't try to talk me out of this. Constance and I are fleeing, and you're coming with us. I'm grown now. At least as much as I will ever be under Hacatine's rule. We're leaving everything behind, aside from what we can carry." He glanced at her and then at the bag he had packed. "Is this too heavy?"

"I think I could handle a few blankets."

The old woman didn't protest like he thought she would. Instead, Claudia smiled at the two. "I think I understand," she said. "You have both waited too long to be together. Much too long."

"Get what you need, mother and let's go. We're headed for the caves. There is work there to be done."

"If that's the case, then I will bring herbs." Claudia pulled a leather pouch off a peg on the wall and took it into the kitchen.

Rummaging lasted only a few minutes. What more did they need but a few clothes, blankets, food and herbs? Constance filled water skins from the well and strung them over her shoulder. Once ready, Abbott led them out the back door of Claudia's thatched roof home onto a deer trail behind the house.

The journey would be slow and dangerous. Abbott could not own a bow, and Claudia's house had been searched regularly for weapons. Aside from the filet knives he had made to carry on his business, they traveled defenseless.

Were it not for Constance's knowledge of the guards and their rotation, making their way to the mountain would be impossible. But she had spent many hours in the woods spinning raftal and used those hours observing as well.

"They congregate at the river when their watches change," she whispered to Abbott.

"And when is that?" he asked.

"Soon. Which means we should find a place in the brush to wait. I'm not sure which trails the warriors have wandered."

Abbott stepped into the low-lying bramble and guided Claudia through the weeds, pulling thorns from her skirt and out of her hair as she passed. Abbott brushed a clearing for her to sit and took a place next to her. Constance found a log across from them and let the strap of a water jug slip off her shoulder. She offered it first to Claudia, who drank sparingly. When she handed the canteen to Abbott, he refused.

"You first."

"How long will it take before they know either of you is missing?" Claudia asked.

"I'm to be in the queen's court at dusk," Constance answered.

"And you, my son?"

Abbott would have been happier not answering, though Claudia would never let him slide. "They are probably looking for me now," he mumbled. Were he alone, he'd have been at the caves by now. He held his fingers to his lips when he heard people on the trail. He recognized their voices. Justine and one woman he had met the day before.

"How far are you going, Viola?"

"I don't know. If we end up having to tell the queen he escaped, she'll have us beat."

"But we've no proof he's missing. Claudia goes to market occasionally. She could very well have been on an errand."

"And where would the wizard-boy be?"

"Fishing maybe, I don't know."

"Come on, Justine. After last night and all that talk about insurrection?"

Claudia gave Abbott a cold, inquiring stare.

"Viola, listen to me." Their talk faded into inaudible whispers and the women eventually left in the direction they had come.

Abbott avoided Claudia's accusing eyes.

"You have a friend in the queen's military, Abbott. Let's take advantage of her generosity while we still can." Constance stood and helped Claudia up. "This place will swarm with guards once dusk comes and they find out that I, too, am missing."

"Will they find the caves?"

"How could they? No. They'll think we descended into the valley to the eastern shores. They'll be looking for us for a very long time."

Abbott slipped quietly through the brush after that, leery to all sounds as the forest grew dense, the path steep. He looked over his shoulder often, worried about Claudia and eager for Constance. If anything happened to either of them, he would never forgive himself.

They reached the cliffs at twilight. No guards wandered the clearing, no deer grazed in the meadow. Only a lone owl's call to its mate interrupted the silence. Beyond the forest edge stood the steep black shale of the mountain wherein the hollows offered safety. Constance moved ahead of Abbott. She had keen eyesight and though her skin glowed an eerie blue in the starlight, and her topaz hair glistened like a doe in winter, she slipped out of sight before even Abbott could focus on her pale form.

"Come," he whispered to Claudia. "Follow her."

"I've been here before, Abbott," Claudia assured him.

Abbott remembered the narrow crevice of the mountain from his childhood. Marked as the beginning of ten years' separation from her, he hated that day. Yet he also knew he'd return. The people who suffered here needed his help. They needed Claudia's help.

Abbott caught up with Constance and took her hand.

"I won't ever let you go, again," he whispered.

"I believe we'll do some good here, Abbott," she answered. "I feel free and fulfilled already. The three of us will make Taikus a better place, beginning with this mountain."

No matter if they had to live in the dark confines of the cave forever, he and Constance would remain as one. Even better that Claudia is with them.

"You've come back," Dante's lanky figure moved into the light, and Abbott saw a smile on his face. "Welcome."

The gentle glow of firelight lit up the faces of the ailing men and women as they stepped into the cavern. The scene as familiar as if he had never left.

Claudia moved toward the beds, resting her pack on the ground and pulling out herbs and oils and tinctures, placing the bottles in a neat row against the cavern wall. Tears streamed down her cheeks as she tended to first one patient, and then another, whispering their names, kissing their hair, touching them. Constance wiped her own eyes with her hands and smiled at Abbott when he turned to her.

"It's good that we came," she said.

Abbott looked into her eyes, glad that they were together, yet the longer he stared the more his heart raced. He turned away.

"What do you see," Constance asked.

She was aware of his gift as much as he was aware of hers, and that is what worried him, for in her eyes were the wings of a butterfly and beyond that a child, and beyond that a dark empty space of loneliness, fire and turmoil.

"It's far into the future," he whispered. "I can't be certain what it is."

Her touch was soft, warm, and loving when she took his head in her hands.

"We will find time to love and heal before the future comes, then, and it will be good."

The End.

The story of Abbott and Constance continues in book 7 of Ian's Realm.

More books in this series

Ian's Realm Trilogy books 1-3

Layla book 4

Diary of a Conjurer Book 5

Cassandra's Castle Book 6

Tale of the Four Wizards

Lost on Taikus

Book 7 coming soon

See also the Sword of Cho Nisi Series

Rise of the Tobian Princess

Fall of the Kings

Curse of Mt Ream

Darkness Holds the Son

The Keeper

To stay up to date with the work of D.L. Gardner, follow her website

https://gardnersart.com

www.ingramcontent.com/pod-product-compliance
Lightning Source LLC
Chambersburg PA
CBHW020919180626
46816CB00007BA/2476

LOST ON TAIKUS

When the young wizard Abbott is abducted as a little boy, he is taken to the castle of the wicked queen Hacatine and condemned to wait his young life as a prisoner until he comes of age and his sentence is executed. But even as a child, Abbott has other plans. When he meets the beautiful albino slave girl who spins silk from a butterfly's spittle he is more determined to not only escape, but bring the entire queen's court with him.

ISBN 978-1-393-33279-4

90000

Frankie & Johnny

LET THE MUSIC PLAY

XIO AXELROD